THE parents BOOK OF BEDTIME STORIES

Edited by TONY BRADMAN

THE parents BOOK OF BEDTIME STORIES

Edited by TONY BRADMAN

Illustrated by SUSIE JENKIN-PEARCE

VIKING KESTREL

VIKING KESTREL

Published by the Penguin Group
27 Wrights Lane, London w8 5TZ, England
Viking Penguin Inc., 40 West 23rd Street, New York, New York 10010, USA
Penguin Books Australia Ltd, Ringwood, Victoria, Australia
Penguin Books Canada Ltd, 2801 John Street, Markham, Ontario, Canada L3R 1B4
Penguin Books (NZ) Ltd, 182–190 Wairau Road, Auckland 10, New Zealand

Penguin Books Ltd, Registered Offices: Harmondsworth, Middlesex, England

This collection first published 1989

Filmset in Linotron Bembo by
Rowland Phototypesetting (London) Ltd.,
30 Oval Road, London NW1 7DE

Printed in Hong Kong by
Imago Publishing Ltd.

A CIP catalogue record for this book is available from the British Library

ISBN 0-670-826251

Contents

Oh No, Matilda!

YSABEL GWYNN

Once, in a wood, there grew a big, old, beautiful tree. And in that tree there lived a family of squirrels – Mum, Dad, Danny, Lucy, and baby Matilda who was a few months old.

Danny and Lucy thought their baby sister was a nuisance. Even though she was very small, she could make an awful lot of noise. And no matter how much noise she made, she was never, ever told off.

Matilda was usually put to bed every night before Danny and Lucy, and by the time they were having their bedtime story with Mum or Dad, she would be fast asleep.

One night, after Mum had kissed Danny and Lucy good-night, she went downstairs to count the hazelnuts left in the larder. She hadn't been gone long when Matilda started to snore. Her snoring was so loud that Danny and Lucy simply couldn't go to sleep.

'Oh no, Matilda!' they said.

Lucy suggested that they go and get Mum and Dad to see if they could do anything to stop her.

'Turn her on to her side,' suggested Dad. They did, but Matilda went right on snoring.

'I'll rub some pine-cone oil on to her chest,' said Mum. It smelt wonderful, but it didn't stop Matilda snoring.

'Let's put a clothes-peg on her nose!' said Danny crossly.

'No, Danny,' said Mum and Dad firmly.

'I know!' cried Lucy. 'I've just remembered – my friend Wriggly Worm always snores. His mum ties a bit of rosemary to his bed, and it works – it stops him snoring!'

So Dad went down the tree, and soon came back with a sprig of rosemary, which he tied to Matilda's cot. And before long, the snores died away.

'Well done, Lucy!' whispered Mum. 'Now – back to bed!' And they all tiptoed away.

They spent the next day sleepily picking hazelnuts, and arrived home late and very tired. 'I hope Matilda doesn't snore tonight,' said Dad, and she didn't; but, just as the children were drifting off to sleep, Matilda suddenly started to sneeze!

'Oh no, Matilda!' cried Danny and Lucy. 'What are we going to do now?'

Mum and Dad tried all sorts of things to stop Matilda sneezing, but they could find nothing that worked.

'Has anyone got any good ideas?' asked Mum. It was getting late and they were all very tired.

'Yes!' said Danny suddenly. 'My junior herbal book has a remedy in it for sneezing! I'll go and get it.' When he came back, they all looked at the recipe for the remedy.

'Good heavens!' said Dad. 'Have we got all those things?'

'I think so,' replied Mum. And she went downstairs with Danny and Lucy to make the remedy. When it was ready, they took it upstairs and gave Matilda a teaspoonful. She stopped sneezing immediately.

'Thank goodness,' whispered the others – and they all tip-toed away and went back to bed.

The next day, very sleepy and cross with Matilda, they

gathered blackberries. Bedtime came at last and the children had just gone off to sleep, when . . . 'Hic! Hic! Hic!'

'Oh no, Matilda!' cried Danny and Lucy, sitting up in bed. 'Now she's got *hiccups*!!'

Even Mum and Dad were a bit annoyed this time. 'What *are* we to do with you, Matilda?' they said.

'Give her a drink of blackberry syrup,' said Dad. But that didn't work.

'How about putting a cold key down her back?' said Mum.

'We know what to do,' said Danny and Lucy together.

They crept out of the room . . . then came back in and shouted, 'BOO!!!'

Mum and Dad weren't sure that Danny and Lucy were right to have shouted *quite* so loud. But at least it worked . . . so they could all tiptoe back to bed.

And it seemed that Matilda was cured completely, for the next night she didn't snore, or sneeze, or hiccup once.

'Thank goodness,' sighed the family as they fell asleep. The tree was lovely and quiet. A breeze blew gently in the branches and stars twinkled in the sky. It was very peaceful . . .

But the following night, just as they were going to sleep, suddenly . . . Matilda went . . .

Snore . . . Aaaatishoo!! Hic! Hic! Hic!

And what did Mum and Dad say, all together?

That's right – 'Oh no, Matilda!'

The Jungle Nursery

TONY KING

Once upon a time, deep in the darkest jungle, there lived a family of gorillas. There was Mum Gorilla, Dad Gorilla, and Baby Gorilla, and they were very happy, except for one thing . . . Baby Gorilla didn't have anyone to play with.

So Mum and Dad decided to start a jungle nursery. They offered to look after all the other animals' children for them so they could do other things. That ought to keep Baby occupied, they thought.

The tigers were the first to arrive the next day. Baby Gorilla thought the tiger cub looked like lots of fun. Tiger Cub took one look at Baby Gorilla, gave a squeaky growl, and started to chase him round and round the jungle clearing.

Soon after, the snakes slid silently from the trees. The snakelets thought Tiger Cub's stripy tail was their long-lost

cousin. They slithered after it, smiling and making friendly hisses, and Tiger Cub chased Baby Gorilla round and round the jungle clearing.

Then the crocodiles crawled out of the river. The tiny crocs thought the snakelets were tasty eels. They scurried after the snakelets, snapping at their wriggling tails, and the snakelets slithered after Tiger Cub, and Tiger Cub chased Baby Gorilla round and round the jungle clearing.

Then the anteaters pushed their way out of the thick undergrowth. Little Anteater thought the bumps on the tiny crocs' tails were ants. She ambled after the tiny crocs, trying to lick the bumps up with her long sticky tongue, and the crocodiles crawled after the snakelets, and the snakelets slid after Tiger Cub, and Tiger Cub chased Baby Gorilla round and round the jungle clearing.

Next came the little monkeys. They scampered up to the top of the trees, giggling and screeching. Then they started to drop squashy, messy fruit on to the little animals below, as they chased each other round and round the jungle clearing.

Next came the baby elephants, who trumpeted, and stamped, and bumped into things as they found all the other baby animals chasing each other round and round the jungle clearing.

Then they all raced off to dive into the river. They splashed, rolled, and wallowed in the warm, squelchy mud of the shallows. Soon you couldn't tell one from another. They were all brown, muddy blobs . . . and then they all came dripping out of the river to chase each other round and round the jungle clearing.

Mum and Dad Gorilla were getting rather cross. 'Stop!' they

shouted. 'Behave yourselves!' they cried. 'It will all end in tears!' But the little animals just kept chasing each other round and round the jungle clearing.

Finally Dad Gorilla lost his temper. He stood up very tall, beat his broad chest with his huge fists, and roared an enormous roar that echoed throughout the jungle. All the jungle creatures heard, and knew it was time to collect their children.

All the mum and dad animals arrived soon, but it wasn't until the elephants had squirted everyone clean with water from their trunks that the parents could tell them apart.

By the time the jungle creatures had taken their children home, it was very late. Mum, Dad, and Baby Gorilla were tired out.

They were just getting into bed when they heard a fluttering, and rustling. Out of the jungle came bats, bush babies, owls, and all the creatures of the night with their children.

'Oh no! Not a night nursery as well,' they groaned, as all the little animals started to chase each other round and round the jungle clearing . . .

Dannie and the Three Bears

SAMANTHA OSBORNE

It was a cold and rainy afternoon. Dannie sat by the window watching the raindrops racing down, all of them in a hurry to be first to the bottom.

He sighed out loud. Oh, I wish I had something exciting to do, he thought.

Mummy was in the kitchen baking cakes for tea. She had told Dannie to read his favourite book – *The Three Bears*. Dannie looked at the book. It had fallen open at the page showing the forest where the three bears lived. He didn't want to read it again. He knew the story off by heart and he knew what was going to happen next.

He wanted something new to do. Dannie looked again at his book, at the same old picture showing high trees and beautiful flowers. But then, to Dannie's surprise, he saw something moving. He peered down at the book and suddenly felt warm sunshine on his face. He looked up. All around him were big trees and pretty flowers.

Why, thought Dannie, this is just like the page in my book.

Dannie gazed about. Up ahead was a little clearing, and Dannie thought he'd walk towards it. As he got closer, Dannie realized that there was a little house there. Once again Dannie thought how strangely similar the house looked to that in his book.

I'll go and see if anyone's at home, he thought, and walked towards the house.

It had a red roof, white walls, and yellow windows with little flowered curtains. There was smoke puffing out of the little chimney.

Dannie knocked on the door. Nobody answered. Dannie knocked again. This time the door opened. There stood Mummy Bear! Dannie couldn't believe his eyes!

'Hello, Dannie,' said Mummy Bear, smiling. 'Won't you come in?'

'How do you know my name?' asked Dannie, wide-eyed.

'You are always reading our story-book,' said Mummy Bear. 'We know all about you – where you live and who your friends are. Now, come inside.'

Dannie followed Mummy Bear. They went into a large kitchen. In a big rocking-chair there sat Father Bear, and playing in the corner was Baby Bear.

'Hello, Dannie,' they both said. 'How nice of you to call. You're just in time for tea.'

Dannie looked around. 'Where's the porridge?' he asked. 'Isn't that what you eat?'

'Oh, no,' laughed Daddy Bear, 'that's just in the story.'

'Oh, I see,' said Dannie, and sat down at the wooden table. Mummy Bear brought over big plates piled high with Dannie's favourite foods: pink ice-cream and red jelly, chocolate cake and jam tarts. Baby Bear came and sat next to Dannie.

'Mmm, my favourite,' he said. 'I love apple pie, don't you?'

'Oh, yes,' said Dannie.

Dannie ate all the good things until he was quite full.

'Let's go and play,' said Baby Bear.

Off they both went to play in the little clearing. Baby Bear knew all the games Dannie did, so they had a great time. First they played hide-and-seek, and then they played hunt the shoe. Dannie was enjoying himself immensely. All of a sudden Mummy Bear shouted to them both to stop playing and come inside. It was getting late and Baby Bear had to go to bed.

Dannie thought it was time he'd better be going.

'Thank you all for such a wonderful time,' he said as he walked back towards the forest.

'Call again soon,' the three bears shouted after him.

Dannie walked into the forest. Once again he noticed a strange thing happening. The trees were getting smaller. The next second Dannie found himself not in the forest but in his own home, and there beside him was his story-book, still open at the forest page.

Just at that very minute Mummy walked in.

'Do you know where I've just been?' asked Dannie, jumping up and running over to her. 'I've just been to the three bears' house for tea.'

Mummy laughed. 'What game have you been playing now?'

'It wasn't a game,' said Dannie. 'I really did go to the three bears' house.'

'Come and have your tea. It's ready now,' said Mummy with a smile.

Dannie went into the kitchen and sat down. Mummy gave him some of the cake she had just made. It was still warm, the way Dannie loved it. But do you know what? Dannie was so full he couldn't eat it.

Dannie wondered. Was it just a dream or did it really happen? He got down from the table and picked up his book. He turned to the page where the three bears were pictured and stared hard at the picture.

But was it his imagination or did Baby Bear give a little wave?

Dannie smiled a secret smile and carefully shut the book.

The Lonely Monster

ANDREW MATTHEWS

The monster woke up. He opened his eyes – one, two, three. He scratched his neck with his claws and stretched his tentacles.

'It's my birthday today!' he roared. 'Happy birthday, monster! Thank you very much!' He had to talk to himself, because he was all alone in the world. Nobody wanted to be friends with a monster as ugly as he was.

Thinking about this made him cry. 'I'm alone!' he sniffed. 'I'm the only lone birthday monster nobody knows!' Tears dripped on to his claws and tickled them until he smiled.

'I'm the only smiling, misery monster I know!'

He jumped to his hooves and his cave shook. 'Shall I sit here, miserabling on this, my birthday day?' he cried. 'No! I'm a cheery monster, I am. Sing me a song, monster. All right, then!'

The monster sang, 'Happy Birthday to Me' so loudly that it made his cave shake, but it didn't stop him from feeling lonely.

'I'm a cheery monster, I am!' shouted the monster. 'I'll make myself a treat for my monstrous birthday tea. Y-A-A-Y!' The monster's larder was a hole in a rock. There was nothing in it but a dead spider and a dried-up slug.

'Curses!' spat the monster. 'Only a dead leggy beastie and a shrivelly slug! I'll have to go into town!'

The monster left his cave and began to stomp down the rocky road. He hadn't gone very far when he heard a noise that made him stop and listen.

'What's this sound, monster? Blessed if I know!'

It was someone singing.

'Happy Birthday to Me.'

The monster thought it was the most beautiful voice he had ever heard. It sounded like an elephant dancing on rusty iron.

The voice was coming from behind a pile of boulders. 'Who's that singing?' shouted the monster.

'Me!' came the reply. 'Who's that shouting?'

'Me!' said the monster.

He walked around the boulders, and there he found a lovely lady monster. Her fur was pink, her scales were purple, and her eyes were blue and red and orange – just like the monster's.

'Why are you singing that song?' the monster asked.

'Because it's my birthday!' wailed the lady monster.

'Nobody wants to be friends with a monster as ugly as me!'

'You're not ugly!' gasped the monster. 'You're a bit of all right, you are! Tell you what – I'll sing "Happy Birthday" to you if you sing "Happy Birthday" to me!'

'Is it your birthday too?' asked the lady monster. 'Fancy me having the same birthday as a hunky big monster like you!'

The monster sang 'Happy Birthday' to the lady monster, and then the lady monster sang 'Happy Birthday' to the monster, and then they did it all over again.

The monster looked at the lady monster and his heart started beating very fast.

'I think we should get married,' he said. 'Will you be Mrs Monster?'

'I certainly will, Mr Monster!' said the lady monster.

And the monster was so pleased that his tail curled up in knots.

Not Till Sunday

TONY BRADMAN

It was the week before Easter, and Tom wondered whether he would be given any lovely chocolate eggs to eat. 'You'll just have to wait and see,' said his dad.

Tom didn't have long to wait.

Monday

On Monday Tom went to playschool. Ben, his best friend, gave him a tiny egg that was all wrapped up in silver paper.

Tom said, 'Thank you very much.'

'Don't eat it till Sunday, now,' said Linda, the playschool lady.

Tuesday

On Tuesday Mrs Smith, the old lady who lived next door, called Tom over to the fence and gave him a little egg with a bow on it.

Tom said, 'Thank you very much.'

'Don't eat it till Sunday, now,' said Mrs Smith.

Wednesday

On Wednesday his big sister didn't tease him, or tell him to get out of her bedroom once . . . and she gave him an egg in a little cup with his name on it. She had bought it with her pocket money.

Tom was surprised, but said, 'Thank you very much.'

'Don't eat it till Sunday, now,' said his sister.

Thursday

On Thursday his aunty came to visit, and brought him a big egg that sat in a hen.

Tom said, 'Thank you very much.'

'Don't eat it till Sunday, now,' said his aunty.

Friday

On Friday his uncle came to visit, and brought him an even bigger egg. This one sat on top of a truck.

Tom thought it looked terrific, but remembered to say . . . 'Thank you very much.'

'Don't eat it till Sunday, now,' said his uncle.

Saturday

On Saturday his granny and grandpa came for lunch, and brought him an egg that was bigger still. They said it had lots of smaller eggs inside it.

Tom thought it looked absolutely wonderful, and said . . . 'Thank you very much.'

'Don't . . .' his granny and grandpa started to say.

'I know,' said Tom. 'Don't eat it till Sunday.'

And, of course, the next day *was* Sunday, Easter Sunday. Tom got one last egg, from his mum and dad, the biggest and most magnificent egg of all. It was so big that Tom could hardly lift it up when he went to put it with the others. 'Thank you [puff] very much [puff].'

Tom counted his Easter eggs. He had one, two, three, four, five, six . . . *seven*. He didn't know where to start. He didn't even think he could eat all of them. Besides, his mum said that if he did, he'd make himself ill. Tom thought that she was probably right.

Then Tom had a very good idea.

On Monday he shared some eggs with Ben, and the other children, and Linda at playschool. *On Tuesday* he shared one with Mrs Smith. *On Wednesday* he shared some with his sister. *On Thursday* he shared with his aunty, *on Friday* with his uncle, and *on Saturday* with Granny and Grandpa.

And everyone said . . . 'Thank you very much.'

Sunday

On Sunday Tom shared the last of his eggs with his mum and dad. That night, as he had done on every other night that week, Dad helped Tom to brush his teeth very, very carefully. And although Tom had enjoyed his lovely chocolate eggs, to tell the truth, he was glad it would be nearly a whole year until it was Easter again.

'I've had enough Easter eggs for now,' he said. 'Thank you very much!'

Donkey Doesn't Like It

THELMA LAMBERT

This is a story about a little girl called Donna and her toy donkey.

Donkey was grey and cuddly with long floppy ears and Donna loved him. Donkey went everywhere with her. And at night he slept nestled up to Donna in her bed. The little girl would pretend that Donkey could talk.

'Donkey doesn't like it!' she would say if they had spinach for dinner.

'Donkey doesn't want to!' she would say when told to go to bed.

Now, one day Mum had to go into hospital. And it was decided that Dad would take Donna to stay with Granny and Grandpa.

'Donkey doesn't want to go to Grandpa's!' said Donna grumpily.

'But they have a little house for the summer, right by the sea!' said Dad. 'You'll love it there.'

Donna had never ever been to the seaside in her life. She asked Mum what it was like, the sea.

'Lovely!' said Mum with a smile. 'Lots and lots of water. Sometimes it's blue and sometimes it's green . . . and there are children paddling, people sailing, fish swimming . . .'

The next morning dawned bright and sunny, and Dad started the car. The little girl and her toy donkey sat in the back looking glum.

It was a very long journey, and Donna was soon fast asleep. When she woke, she saw out of the window lots and lots of green water. And there were children paddling. Donna thought, this must be the seaside!

'No!' laughed Dad. 'It's only a big pond!'

They drove on. Donna fell asleep a second time. And when she woke, she saw out of the window lots and lots of *blue* water, and people sailing boats. This *must* be the sea, thought Donna.

But Dad said no, it was just a lake. Donna slept once more, and this time she woke up because Dad had stopped the car.

'We're there!' cried Dad.

Stiffly Donna climbed out of the car and rubbed her eyes. But she couldn't see any water at all. Just sand as far as the eye could see.

'Where is it?' she said. 'I can't see any sea!'

Dad pointed. Sparkling in the sun, far, far away, was a thin silver line. *That* was the sea! The tide had gone so far out there was only an enormous beach left.

'Donkey doesn't like it,' said Donna. 'It's too big. Too much sand!'

But just then two things happened to make Donna change her mind. Donkey too.

The first thing was that Donna saw – walking slowly across the sand – Granny and Grandpa! They were wearing their straw sun-hats. Grandpa was bringing ice-creams for everyone!

The other thing that happened was that from the opposite direction came – walking slowly across the sand – two donkeys! They had grey hair, just like Granny and Grandpa, and they wore straw sun-hats too. But their hats had little holes for their ears to poke through!

'LOOK, Donkey! Here are YOUR Granny and Grandpa!' exclaimed Donna. 'You've come to visit THEM!'

That night in the cosy little house by the sea Donna and Donkey snuggled down in a warm bed. Granny came in to kiss them goodnight.

'I was thinking,' said Granny. 'Would Donkey like me to make him a little sun-hat, like the real donkeys have on the beach?'

Donna said he definitely *would*.

'Granny! I think I'm going to like it here!' said Donna, tucking the blanket round her toy donkey. 'And Donkey says he likes it too!'

The Witch Who Asked the Way

HAZEL TOWNSON

Georgе had had a busy day and was tired. It was lovely to lie in bed and look forward to an exciting dream. He closed his eyes – but they soon flew open again. For George had heard a swishing noise outside his window.

He climbed out of bed, pulled back the curtains, and was just in time to see a witch flying by on her broomstick!

When the witch saw George, she flew back and tapped on his window. 'Excuse me, but I'm looking for Rosemary Cottage. Can you direct me?'

George leaned out of the window. 'It's right here!' said George, for Rosemary Cottage was the house he lived in.

'Well, wallop me withershins!' cried the witch. 'Then you must be young George?'

'That's right,' said George.

'I'm supposed to put a spell on you,' said the witch. 'What do you think of that?'

'Is it a good spell, or a bad one?' asked George.

'Well, now, that depends on how you behave yourself,' said the witch. 'If you're willing to risk it, climb up behind me.'

'All right,' said George, who could not resist such a wonderful adventure. The ride on the broomstick was fun. George felt like a shooting star. At last they swooped down beside a little wooden house, and the witch took George inside.

There were three black cats sitting in a row on the sofa.

'Sit on the end of the sofa,' said the witch. 'You like cats, don't you?'

'Oh, certainly!' said George, sitting down at once. 'I have a cat of my own called Silversocks.'

The first cat purred and came to sit on George's lap.

'And do you like weed-and-tadpole stew?' asked the witch, stirring a cauldron on the fire.

'Oh, certainly!' said George. 'I once fell into a pond full of weeds and tadpoles and I gulped down a lot of the water. It was delicious.'

The second cat purred and came over to rub its back against George's leg.

'And do you like WITCHES?' asked the witch, grinning a great, crooked grin.

'Oh, certainly!' said George. 'For if I hadn't met you, I'd never have had this adventure.'

The third cat purred and jumped up on to George's shoulder.

'Well, wallop me withershins!' cried the witch. 'For we all like *you* too!' So saying, she took a great pair of scissors from the table and cut off a lock of George's hair. She threw this into the stew and stirred it up, muttering some magic words, while the three cats purred and purred. Then the witch took a tiny bottle and filled it from a deep ladle which she dipped in the cauldron. She gave the bottle to George.

'If ever you can't sleep,' she said, 'put three drops of that on your tongue. You'll fall asleep at once, and you will have the very dream you'd most enjoy. Now, it's time you went home.'

So George said goodbye to the cats and rode back with the witch on her broomstick. Then he climbed in through his bedroom window and back to bed. After such an adventure George was too excited to fall asleep, so he tried three drops of the witch's spell, and it worked. He fell asleep at once and had the most wonderful dream.

At breakfast next morning George told his mum and dad all that had happened, but they did not believe him.

'Don't make up silly stories, George,' said Mum.

Then Dad said, 'Here, young George, why have you cut off a lock of your hair?'

The Persistent Snail

LINDA ALLEN

Once there was a very old woman who grew lettuces in her garden. Every morning she watered them, and every afternoon she picked one for her tea.

One day she went out to water her lettuces and found that they had been nibbled around the edges. 'Snails!' she cried. 'There are snails in my garden nibbling my lettuces!' The old woman searched for snails all day, but she did not find any.

In fact there was only one snail in her garden, but he had a very big appetite. On his shell was a curious mark, like the wings of a butterfly. No other snail had a shell like his.

He only came out at night. In the day he stayed fast asleep in a hole in the wall.

That night the old woman went out with a lantern to look for him. She found him nibbling one of her lettuces. 'So it's you!' she said. 'I knew I would catch you by the light of my lantern.'

She was a kind old woman who never killed anything, so she put the snail in a box and carried him out into the lane. She walked along the lane for a mile until she came to a garden wall. 'There you are,' she said to the snail. 'I am sure you will find something to eat around here. Goodbye and good luck to you!' Then she went home.

At first the snail was rather confused. But he could smell something delicious not very far away. He slid down the wall and went to look for it. In the garden behind the wall he found the most scrumptious cabbages he had ever tasted.

In the morning the old man who lived there came out to look at his cabbages. 'Snails!' he shouted. 'There are snails in my garden eating my cabbages.' But there was only one snail . . . who had found a hole in the wall and was fast asleep. The old man couldn't find him.

That night the old man went out with a lantern and searched. At last he found the snail with the curious mark on his shell. 'It's you!' he cried. 'You'd better come with me.'

He put the snail in his pocket and walked a mile up the lane until he came to the old woman's garden wall. 'There you are,' he said, taking the snail out of his pocket. 'Eat what you find in there and don't you trouble me again.' Then he went home.

Next morning the old woman went to water her lettuces. 'Another snail!' she said. 'Well, I will find him tonight, and then I'll take him to where I took the other one I found.'

She was amazed to find that it was the very same snail. 'How did you get back here so quickly?' she said. 'I never knew that snails could travel so fast.' Once again she put him in the box and carried him along the lane. The next night the old man found him again and took him back. And so it went on, for a week or even more.

One day the old man and the old woman met in the lane. It was raining. 'I am glad it is raining,' said the old woman. 'I shall not have to water my lettuces today.'

'And I shall not have to water my cabbages,' said the old man. Then he told the old woman what had been happening to him.

'That's very odd!' exclaimed the old woman. 'The very same thing has been happening to me.'

'What does your snail look like?' asked the old man.

'Oh,' said the old woman, 'he has a mark on his shell like the wings of a butterfly.'

'So has my snail,' cried the old man.

Then they started to laugh. 'It is the very same snail!' they said. 'What shall we do?'

The old man had an idea. 'Well,' he said, 'the little snail seems to enjoy my cabbages just as much as he enjoys your lettuces. I will grow a row of cabbages specially for him, if you will grow a row of lettuces for him too.'

'Oh, I'm sure he would like that!' laughed the old woman. 'And every week we will meet in the lane and hand him over. He will eat cabbage one week and lettuce the next.'

The snail was delighted with the arrangement. It isn't every snail who has two homes, and he used to look forward to his trip down the lane every week.

As for the old man and the old woman, they became the very best of friends. And all because of the little snail who would not go away.

Jack and the Friendly Dentist

JENNIFER CURRY

R ight!' said Jack's mum. 'It's eleven o'clock. Off you go and give your teeth a really good brush. Up and down. Inside and out. And when you've finished that, you can do it all over again.'

Jack looked at the hands of the big kitchen clock, and then he looked at his mum. There was something wrong somewhere. 'Eleven o'clock is not teeth-brushing time,' he said. 'It's going-out-shopping time.'

His mum laughed. 'Today's different,' she explained. 'Today it is teeth-brushing time, and THEN – it's going-to-the-dentist time.'

'No!' said Jack. 'Don't want to.'

But it was no good. His mum pounced on him, tucked him under her arm, and carried him off, squealing and struggling, to the bathroom.

'The dentist won't hurt you,' she said. 'She's just going to look at your teeth to make sure they are all clean and healthy.'

'Don't LIKE the dentist!' grunted Jack, trying to wriggle free.

'What nonsense!' exclaimed his mum. 'You're just being silly!'

Jack opened his mouth to argue – and straight away his mum had the toothbrush in there and was scrubbing away like billy-o. He tried to complain, but there was no way he could utter as much as a squeak, so he just had to put up with it.

The dentist's surgery was in a big old house in a quiet road behind the High Street. Jack's mum opened the black front door, then they went through another door with RECEPTION written on it. Inside, Jack saw a lady in a white coat.

'Are you the dentist?' he asked.

She laughed and shook her head. 'I'm the receptionist,' she said. 'I look after people before they see the dentist.' Then she turned to Jack's mum. 'I'm afraid he'll have to wait about twenty minutes,' she said. 'We've been so busy we are running late this morning.'

'Never mind,' said Jack's mum. 'We can wait, can't we, Jack?'

'No!' said Jack. 'Don't want to.'

The receptionist pointed to the corner of the room. 'Look, there are some toys over there.'

On the floor there were all sorts of exciting things. It was just like Christmas Day. There was a big wooden box with holes in the sides so you could either crawl right through it, climb on to the top of it, or sit inside it. It was great. And there was a bouncy clown who just wouldn't fall over no matter how hard you pushed him. But the thing Jack liked best of all was a yellow duck you could sit on and rock backwards and forwards.

'Off you go and play,' said his mum.

But Jack shook his head. He really would have liked a ride on that yellow duck, but he couldn't let his mum think he was actually enjoying being at the dentist's.

So . . . 'No!' said Jack. 'Don't want to.'

For five long minutes Jack sat on a chair, swinging his legs and looking out of the window. He felt bored. And miserable. And a bit frightened about what the dentist would do to him.

'You could go out into the garden if you liked,' said the receptionist. 'There's a swing.'

Jack was just opening his mouth to say, 'No! Don't want to', when he saw his mum giving him one of her looks, so he thought he'd better change his mind. 'OK,' he said, and followed the receptionist out through the back door into a sunny garden.

'I'll call you when it's time,' she said, and left him there.

Just as Jack had decided that he really would like a go on the swing, he saw a little girl running towards it. 'Hey!' he shouted. 'It's my go first.'

The girl turned round and waved at him. It was Amy Craggs, who went to his playschool. 'Hello!' she said. 'Do you want to play on my swing?'

'It's not your swing,' said Jack.

'It *is* my swing,' said Amy. 'And this is my garden.'

'It's not your garden,' said Jack. 'It's the dentist's. Have you come to see the dentist? You'll have to wait, they're running late!'

Amy giggled and shook her head. 'I live here,' she said.

'No you don't. The dentist lives here.'

'I know.' Amy giggled again. 'The dentist is my mum.'

Jack was astonished. It must be very peculiar to have a dentist for a mum, he thought. But Amy was always laughing and fooling around, so she must think it was OK. He was just opening his mouth to ask Amy whether her mum hurt her when she was looking at her teeth, when the receptionist called him. 'Come along, Jack,' she said. 'Mrs Craggs will see you now.'

'No!' said Jack. 'Don't want to.' But then he saw Amy laughing at him again, so he changed his mind and marched bravely into the surgery.

Amy's mum was all right really, Jack decided. She sat him in a funny chair and made it go up, then down, then tip over backwards so quickly that he couldn't help giggling. Then, when she was looking at his teeth, she told him how she had laughed at the school concert when he and Amy had sung 'Jack and Jill' and he'd had to fall down on the stage with his pail. When she had finished poking about in his mouth with her little silver stick, she looked pleased. 'Very good!' she said. 'You deserve a reward for splendid teeth like that.' And, opening her cupboard, she took out a big round red balloon. It had a picture on it of a smiling mouth, with lots and lots of flashing white teeth.

'What does it say?' Jack asked, pointing to the words underneath the picture.

Mrs Craggs laughed. 'It says, "MY TEETH ARE THE GREATEST!"'

Jack felt very proud of himself as he followed his mum out of the black front door and into the road again, carrying the red balloon.

'That was all right!' he said. 'You don't need to worry, Mum. Going to the dentist's is OK.'

What's Wrong with Gerry Gerbil?
A. H. BENJAMIN

One day Katie came home from school and, as always, she went straight to her bedroom to see her pet gerbil.

'Hi, Gerry!' she chirped, her face close to the cage.

Usually Gerry answered her with squeaks of delight. Then, to show how clever he was, he would hop into his wheel and start running like mad. But today he didn't. Head tucked between his paws, he just lay in a corner of his cage looking very miserable.

'Hey, why do you look so sad?' asked Katie. Concerned, she took him out of the cage and held him close to her, gently stroking his soft fur.

Just then her mother walked into the room. 'Something wrong?' she asked.

'It's Gerry,' replied Katie. 'I can't understand why he's so sad. He didn't even go in his wheel for me.'

'Don't fret, love,' her mother reassured her. 'Maybe he's just tired.'

Katie didn't think so, but she said nothing.

At the dinner table she hardly touched her food, she was so worried. What could be wrong with Gerry, she kept wondering. There must be something making him sad.

Timmy, Katie's younger brother, thought he knew. 'Gerry ate too much and now his tummy hurts!' he piped.

Frowning, Katie looked at her father. 'Do you think Gerry has an ingidestion?' she asked.

'You mean indigestion,' corrected her father, smiling. 'Oh, er – it's possible. Anyway, if Gerry has one, it should go away soon.'

'I still say that he's just tired,' said her mother.

Katie cheered up a bit. Maybe she was worrying for nothing.

However, when she went to see Gerry later on, she found him looking sadder than ever. And no matter how hard she tried to coax him to go in his wheel, he just wouldn't. Very upset, Katie began to cry.

'I tell you what,' said her mother soothingly. 'There is no school tomorrow, it's Saturday. We'll take Gerry to the vet first thing in the morning.'

And they did.

'Mmm, strange,' said the vet when they had told him what

the trouble was. 'Perhaps he's hurt a leg . . . or pulled a muscle. Anyway, I'll soon find out.'

Katie watched anxiously as the vet began to examine Gerry. Supposing he'd hurt a leg badly, she wondered. Maybe he would never be able to go in his wheel again. Just thinking about it brought tears to her eyes.

To her relief the vet said, 'I can't find anything wrong with him. Nothing at all.' Even he looked bewildered.

Once back home, Katie went to her bedroom. She sat beside Gerry's cage, looking just as sad as he did. Why should Gerry suddenly stop going in his wheel, she kept asking herself, puzzled. Surely there must be a reason. She was so busy thinking that she didn't hear Timmy come into the room . . . until he dropped a small toy wheelbarrow by her feet.

'It's broken!' he said sulkily. 'The wheel doesn't go round!'

'Leave me alone,' said Katie, not in the mood for company.

'The wheel doesn't go round!' repeated Timmy. 'The wheel doesn't go round!'

'Go away!' Katie told him, annoyed. But just then she realized what Timmy was saying. A thought occurred to her: could Gerry's wheel . . . Quickly she opened the cage's door. She tried to turn the wheel round with her finger, and couldn't. It was firmly jammed!

'No wonder!' she cried. 'So *that*'s why you wouldn't go in your wheel!' she said to Gerry.

Carrying the cage in her arms, she rushed downstairs to tell her father and mother. 'Please, Daddy, can you mend it?' she begged breathlessly.

'Of course,' agreed her father, and in no time he had the wheel cleaned and oiled. 'There,' he said. 'It's as good as new now.'

Trembling with excitement, Katie put Gerry back in his cage. 'Your wheel is all right now,' she told him. 'Look, Gerry!' And she turned it round with her finger.

Squeaking with delight, Gerry at once scurried into his wheel. Oh, the joy on his face as he ran faster and faster. He must have missed it terribly, because he just would not stop running.

'Look at him go, look at him!' cried Katie, clapping and jumping up and down with glee. She felt so happy she grabbed Timmy and gave him a big hug. 'It was all thanks to you!' she said to him. '*You* made me think of the wheel!'

Timmy beamed, and then he proudly shouted, 'The wheel doesn't go round!'

The Unscary Spider

DAWN COOK

Sidney is a big black spider. He has a large hairy body and eight long hairy legs, and he lives in the cupboard under the stairs.

Now, Sidney looks very, very scary. Scary enough to frighten the tallest giants, and the largest monsters. But the only trouble is, poor Sidney doesn't actually scare anybody.

He tried to scare the children that live in the house, but they just looked at him and laughed. He tried to scare the children's mummy, who lives in the house, but she just swept him out into the garden. He tried to scare the children's daddy, who also lives in the house, but he just washed him down the plughole. He tried to scare the dog that lives in the house, but he just barked and growled at him. He tried to scare the cat that lives in the house, but he just hissed and spat and chased him back into the cupboard.

Poor Sidney was so sad. He just couldn't scare anything. He sat in his cupboard and cried. Night-time came, and Sidney was still sitting in his cupboard. 'I've got a good idea!' he said to himself. 'I'll go for a walk around the house. Perhaps I will be more scary in the dark.'

Sidney came out of his cupboard and started to walk – into the kitchen, into the living-room, into the bedrooms. But no one was about; they had all gone to bed.

'Oh well, never mind!' said Sidney. 'I suppose I shall just have to go back to the cupboard to sleep.'

Just as he was walking back home, he saw a light on in the bathroom. Aha, thought Sidney, maybe there is someone in here that I can scare! And he went in.

There was no one in there. Except!!

Sidney turned round quickly, and there, staring at him, was a big black spider.

'EEK!! ARGG!!' shouted Sidney. 'Help, help!' And he ran out of the bathroom.

You see, Sidney saw himself in the bathroom mirror. But at last he had scared someone. He'd scared HIMSELF.

Pogo the Ogre

HAZEL TOWNSON

An ogre is a man-eating monster that looks like a bad-tempered giant.

Pogo was an ogre, but he was very finicky with his food. He did not like the taste of man.

When Pogo was little, his mother used to say to him at breakfast-time, 'Come on, now, eat up your nice shredded man!'

But Pogo just pulled a face and pushed his dish away.

Then Pogo's father would say, 'Right! He'll get that man served up again at lunch-time and tea-time and supper-time until he eats it!'

Yet all that happened was that Pogo pulled a worse face at every meal and pushed his dish even further away.

Well, Pogo grew as thin as a clothes-line because he was living on nothing but lettuce and lily-pads and lotus leaves. All his neighbours began to laugh and sneer and call him Pogo Stick.

When the time came for the Ogre Olympics, Pogo's neighbours sniggered even louder. They were all in training, busy building up their muscles and feeding on ogre-sized man-steaks until they were all so big and strong they felt sure they could never be beaten. Pogo just flopped around and read his comics.

The ogres' training programme was hard on the villagers of Witsend nearby, for, of course, more and more of them were snatched away daily to be turned into ogres' dinners. At last the villagers decided on a plan. The ogres might have all the muscle, but the villagers had all the brains.

First they persuaded Pogo to get up early in the mornings and jog round the park. Several of them jogged along with him to make sure he didn't cheat. Then they made him do knee-bends and press-ups, and cycle and skip. Best of all, Caleb the Cobbler made Pogo some special running shoes that were the springiest in the world, and Thomas the Tailor made Pogo a tickly vest, some tickly shorts and a track-suit with a built-in Energy Booster.

Pogo's name was entered for the 100 kilometres, the 200 kilometres, the hop-step-and-jump, the hurdles, and the marathon. All the other ogres laughed and thought that Pogo could never hope to finish the course, let alone win. That little wimp! How dared he even enter the contests?

But they were in for a shock. At the start of each race Pogo's outfit tickled him so much that he ran like an escaping convict towards the giant bottle of ANTI-TICK-LING LOTION that the villagers of Witsend were holding up at the winning-post. First Pogo won the 100 kilometres, then the 200 kilometres, then the hop-step-and-jump, then the hurdles. As for the marathon, Pogo chased home with half an hour to spare before the next ogre staggered in. In fact only one other ogre finished the race at all. Most of them collapsed from exhaustion.

In the end there were so many dying ogres strewn about the place that there were not enough ogre doctors to go round. Donald the Doctor from Witsend had to be called in.

Donald tutted and sadly shook his head.

'You are killing yourselves off!' he said. Surely the ogres could see that it was far healthier to eat up their greens, as Pogo did, and cut down on the man-meat.

'Every time you kill one of us for food, you are killing yourselves as well,' he warned. 'But there are more of us than there are of you. So you will soon be extinct, while we shall live to tell the tale.'

But the ogres did not listen. And that is why there are no more ogres left in the world. Except for Pogo, of course. He is already 192 years old, so he looks like going on for ever.

The Monster's Cake

ANDREW MATTHEWS

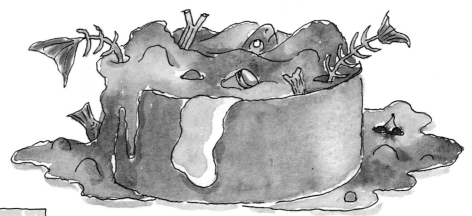

Mrs Monster combed her tentacles, dusted her wings, and brushed her tails. 'My monstrous husband has gone off to the forest to make some furniture for the cave!' she said to herself. 'I'm going to give him a super special treat when he gets in! After a hard day's furniture making, there's nothing a hungry monster likes better than a great big cake!'

Chuckling with glee at her good idea, Mrs Monster looked into the larder. There were all sorts of packets and tins and jars in there.

'I wonder what goes into a cake?' said Mrs Monster. 'I know! I'll put in everything we both like! Only the best for Mr Monster!'

Mrs Monster took a huge bowl and started to put things into it. As she worked, she made up a poem about mixing the cake.

'In goes honey, in goes jam!
In goes flour and a slice of ham!
In goes rhubarb, in goes rice!
In goes salmon, in goes spice!
In go cherries, salt, and mustard,
Clotted cream and grapes and custard!
In go curry and tomato sauce,
Yoghurt and chocolate – and sugar, of course!
Mix 'em in, mix 'em out,
Turn 'em round and round about!'

When she came to the mixing part, Mrs Monster grabbed hold of a giant wooden spoon and stirred so fast that quite a lot of mixture fell on to the floor of the cave.

'That should do the trick!' said Mrs Monster happily. 'Looks all right! Smells a bit funny, though! Still, I expect it'll smell different when it's cooked.'

It was time to light the stove. Mrs Monster threw in plenty of logs, then breathed on them with her fiery monster breath. HOOSH! HOOSH! HOOSH!

Before long the stove was glowing red hot. Mrs Monster picked up the bowl and threw it into the roaring flames. But, instead of turning into a cake, the mixture in the bowl went bubbly, then black, and then vanished in a puff of smoke and fire.

'Oh, no! Where's Mr Monster's surprise cake?' shouted Mrs Monster.

She was so upset that she cried big tears. They fell on to the stove and put it out. The cave was filled with smoke and steam.

'Who's that crying?' someone screeched. It was Mr Monster.

In a sniffy sort of voice, Mrs Monster told him about the surprise cake.

'Well, I'm no good at making furniture,' said Mr Monster. He held up his claws to show his wife the bandages on them. 'I keep hitting myself with the hammer,' he explained miserably.

'But making furniture's easy-peasy!' gasped Mrs Monster. 'My old granny showed me how.'

'That's funny!' laughed Mr Monster. 'My old granny showed me how to bake cakes! Tell you what, from now on you make the furniture and I'll do the cooking!'

'Right!' roared Mrs Monster.

And from that day on Mr Monster wore a pinafore and cooked all the meals, while Mrs Monster wore overalls and made tables and chairs.

And it was great.

The Real Father Christmas

TONY BRADMAN

'Come on, Tom,' said Dad. 'It's time to go. You don't want to be late for your party, do you?'

Tom was going to the Christmas party at his playgroup. He had been looking forward to it for weeks . . . but now he wasn't all that interested any more.

'Put your coat on, Tom,' said Dad. 'That's it . . . If we don't get a move on, you won't be there when Father Christmas arrives. And that will be really exciting, won't it?'

It *would* have been exciting . . . if it had been the *real* Father Christmas. Tom knew it wouldn't be, though. It would be his friend Josie's dad, dressed up in a hired Santa Claus costume.

Josie had come to play at Tom's house last night. That's when she had told him about the costume she had found in her parents' bedroom.

'There was a big red coat, and red trousers, and a false beard. I heard my mum and dad talking about it, too,' she had said. 'So there isn't a real Father Christmas at all. It's just a story mums and dads tell children.'

'It isn't!' Tom had said. But he wasn't so sure. And that made him feel really fed up. He had wanted to ask Father Christmas for a special present, a fantastic red car he'd seen in the toyshop. He hadn't told anyone he wanted it, not even Mum or Dad. And now he'd never get it.

It didn't take Tom and his dad long to get to playgroup. Tom took off his coat and hung it on his special peg, the one with his name underneath.

'Hello, Tom,' said Linda, the playgroup lady. 'In you come . . .' Tom's dad gave him a kiss and said goodbye.

Tom looked around. All his friends were there already . . . except Josie. She's bound to arrive with Father Christmas, he thought.

They had put up some decorations, and there was a Christmas tree in the corner by the piano. Tom noticed there was a chair next to it, too.

'That's where Father Christmas is going to sit,' said Linda. Just then there was a knock on the door.

'I wonder who that could be?' said Linda. 'It's a little too early for Father Christmas . . .'

But that's exactly who it was. Linda opened the door, and

there in front of her was a large man with a huge white beard, all dressed in red.

'Merry Christmas!' he said in a loud voice. Then he called out to someone, or something, behind him. 'Stay there, Rudolph, I won't be long . . . Stop that, Prancer! Behave yourself!'

'Oh . . . er, Merry Christmas,' said Linda. 'You'd better come in.'

Tom looked closely, but he had to admit it didn't look much like Josie's dad. The man looked just like . . . Father Christmas.

He marched into playgroup, strode over to the chair, and dumped a big, bulging sack in front of him.

'Merry Christmas, children!' he called out in his booming voice. He smiled, and everyone smiled back. 'Merry Christmas!' they all said.

'Right, who's first?' he said. One by one the children went up to him. He chatted to them for a while and gave each one a present. He laughed a lot and made everyone feel really happy.

At last it was Tom's turn. He looked up at the man's twinkling eyes.

'Hello, Tom,' he said.

'Hello,' said Tom. Then he couldn't stop himself. 'You're not the *real* Father Christmas, are you?' he said.

'Ho, ho, ho!' laughed the man. 'I *feel* real enough. Why don't you pull my beard and see if it comes off?'

He bent down, smiling. Tom gave his beard a tug, but it didn't come off. The man gave him his present.

'I think it's what you want, Tom. But don't unwrap it until Christmas Day . . .' he said with a wink. 'Well, I must be off. I've got to get back to the North Pole tonight . . . Cheerio, everyone!'

'Say goodbye to Father Christmas, children!' said Linda.

They all said goodbye, and the man left, waving. It was very cold outside, so Linda shut the door behind him quickly. Tom wasn't sure, but he *thought* he heard the sound of bells tinkling and the man shouting something like 'Heigh-ho, Rudolph . . .'

Linda said they were going to have a story next. But, just as they settled down in the book corner, there was a knock on the door.

'Now, who can it be this time?' said Linda. She went to the door and opened it. And there in front of her was . . . another Father Christmas, with Josie standing next to him.

'I'm sorry I'm late,' whispered the second Father Christmas. 'But the car broke down, and we had to walk . . .'

Tom knew it was Josie's dad. It looked just like him.

'But I don't understand . . .' Linda was saying. 'You've already been and gone!'

The second Father Christmas looked confused. 'I haven't,' he said.

'Well, if it wasn't you who came earlier,' said Linda, 'who was it?'

Tom smiled. He knew who it had been. And he had a pretty good idea what his present was, too . . .